WALT DISNEY PRODUCTIONS
presents

Robin Hood
AND THE
Birthday Penny

Random House New York

Book Club Edition

First American Edition. Copyright © 1982 by Walt Disney Productions. All rights reserved under International and Pan-American Copyright Conventions. Published in the United States by Random House, Inc., New York, and simultaneously in Canada by Random House of Canada Limited, Toronto. Originally published in Denmark as ROBIN HOOD HJAELPER SKIPPY by Gutenberghus Gruppen, Copenhagen. Copyright © 1981 by Walt Disney Productions. ISBN: 0-394-84845-4
1234567890   ABCDEFGHIJK

It was Skippy Rabbit's birthday.
"Happy birthday, Skippy!"
said his family.

And it WAS a happy birthday—
even though there was no money
for a cake.

Mother Rabbit gave Skippy a present.
Skippy opened it.
"A penny! Oh, thank you!"
he said happily.

Just then the sheriff came in
to collect money for Prince John.
He grabbed Skippy's penny!
"Hey, this penny is bent," he said.

"But a bent penny is still money,"
said the sheriff. "And all money belongs
to Prince John."

He put the penny in his pocket and left.

A few minutes later Robin Hood came in.
"Why is everyone so sad?" he asked.
"The sheriff took my birthday penny,"
said Skippy. "A special bent penny."

"Cheer up, Skippy," said Robin.
"I've brought you a birthday present—
a bow and arrows!"

"Wow!" said Skippy. "Now I can be
a great archer—just like you!"

Skippy was very proud.
"You need one more thing,"
said Robin.
He gave Skippy a hat.
"Perfect!" everyone said.

Robin hung up a target outdoors.
He showed Skippy how to shoot arrows.

Nearby, Prince John was floating on
a raft with his servant, Sir Hiss.
But Robin and Skippy could not see them.

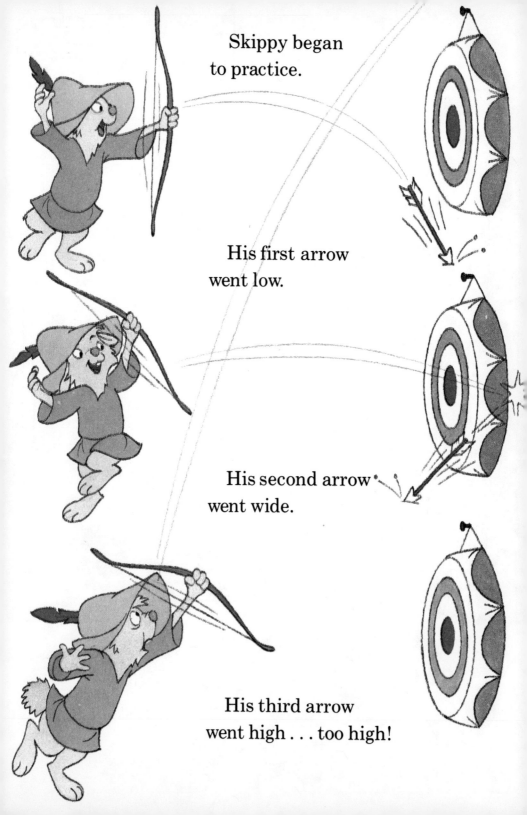

Skippy began
to practice.

His first arrow
went low.

His second arrow
went wide.

His third arrow
went high . . . too high!

The arrow went right over the wall.
It hit Prince John's raft.
WHOOSH! Out went the air.
The raft began to sink!

"I'm drowning!" yelled Prince John.
Sir Hiss said, "The water is not
that deep, sire."

"BE QUIET!" said Prince John.
"If I say I'm drowning, I'm drowning!"

Robin Hood heard the shouting.
"Run home, quickly!" he told Skippy.

"Who shot
that arrow?
Lift me up
so I can see!"
the prince said
to his guards.

Prince John looked
over the wall and saw
Robin Hood.
"I was just leaving,"
said Robin. "Toodle-loo!"

Prince John was very angry.
"Find Robin Hood! Put him in jail!"
he told his sheriff.

Robin Hood lived in Sherwood Forest.
The sheriff went there with his men.
They looked everywhere for Robin.

But they could not find him.
Robin and his friend Little John
knew all the good hiding places.

Robin and Little John knew that
Prince John took money from poor people.
They made a plan to get the money back.
Then they set out—each a different way.

Soon Little John met a pie seller.

"I will give you a bag of gold for your pies, your cart, and your clothes," said Little John.

The pie seller said, "It's a deal!"

Little John put on the pie seller's clothes.
Then he pushed the pie cart into town.

What was Little John going to do?
He was going to fool the prince.
He wanted Prince John to think
that he had lots of money.

So Little John did not SELL
his pies.

He gave them away!

Prince John watched him
hand out the pies.

The prince was VERY surprised!

"That pie seller must be very rich,"
said Prince John. "He doesn't even
have to sell his pies!"

"Is he as rich as you?" asked Sir Hiss.
The prince said, "We will see!"

The prince sent for the pie seller.
"Do you have a safe place to hide
your money?" asked the prince.
"Sure—Sherwood Forest," Little John
said. "Even Robin Hood can't find it!"

"I would like to see a place THAT safe!"
cried the prince.

"I will show it to you," said Little John.

Then the prince whispered to Sir Hiss,
"We will take this stupid pieman's money!"

They all set out in the royal coach.
The sheriff and his men came too.
Prince John took his gold along.
"You should leave your gold at home,"
Sir Hiss told the prince. "Robin Hood
will try to take it!"

"Nonsense!" said the prince.
"I never go anywhere without my gold."

They came to the middle
of the forest.

There stood a magician.

It was Robin Hood in
magician's clothes!

"Tricks for a penny,"
called Robin.

"Don't stop, sire," begged Sir Hiss.
"Robin Hood may be near."

"Be quiet!" said the prince. "I love
magic tricks. Sheriff, give that man
a penny!"

The sheriff handed Robin a coin.
It was Skippy's bent penny.

Suddenly Little John called out,
"Robin Hood is coming! I see him!
Hide your gold, Prince John!"

"It's a trick!" said Sir Hiss.

"Nonsense!" said the prince. "Pie seller,
tell me where to hide my gold!"

"Give me the gold,"
said Little John.
"I will hide it
for you."

"Here! Take it! Hurry!" said the prince.
He gave his bags of gold to Little John.
"Fear not!" said Little John. "I will
treat this gold like my own!"

Little John ran off
into the forest.

The magician said,
"Sheriff, here is your
chance to be a hero.
Catch Robin Hood!"
The sheriff said,
"I want my penny back!"
"Forget the penny!"
yelled the prince.
"Go catch Robin!"

The sheriff and his men
raced into the forest.

Then Robin Hood took off
his magician's clothes.

Prince John and Sir Hiss
had a royal surprise.

"I was just leaving,"
said Robin.
He tipped his hat.
"Toodle-loo!"

"Robin Hood has tricked
me!" cried Prince John.
"I'll never see my gold again!"
"I tried to warn you,"
said Sir Hiss.
"Oh, be quiet!" said
the prince.

Robin Hood and Little John did not
keep the gold.

They gave it back to the poor people.

Robin took one bag to the rabbit family.
He also brought a birthday cake for Skippy.
All the rabbits were so happy!

Then Robin gave Skippy his bent penny.
"I have my penny back!" said Skippy.
"This is the best birthday ever!"
And it was, thanks to Robin Hood.